Learning to Read, Step by Step!

Ready to Read **Preschool–Kindergarten**
• big type and easy words • rhyme and rhythm • picture clues
For children who know the alphabet and are eager to begin reading.

Reading with Help **Preschool–Grade 1**
• basic vocabulary • short sentences • simple stories
For children who recognize familiar words and sound out new words with help.

Reading on Your Own **Grades 1–3**
• engaging characters • easy-to-follow plots • popular topics
For children who are ready to read on their own.

Reading Paragraphs **Grades 2–3**
• challenging vocabulary • short paragraphs • exciting stories
For newly independent readers who read simple sentences with confidence.

Ready for Chapters **Grades 2–4**
• chapters • longer paragraphs • full-color art
For children who want to take the plunge into chapter books but still like colorful pictures.

STEP INTO READING® is designed to give every child a successful reading experience. The grade levels are only guides; children will progress through the steps at their own speed, developing confidence in their reading.

Remember, a lifetime love of reading starts with a single step!

This book is dedicated to
all the big people who are
helping smaller people
learn to read.
The StoryBots love you!

Designed by Greg Mako

© 2021 Netflix, Inc.

All rights reserved. Published in the United States by Random House Children's Books, a division of Penguin Random House LLC, 1745 Broadway, New York, NY 10019, and in Canada by Penguin Random House Canada Limited, Toronto.

Step into Reading, Random House, and the Random House colophon are registered trademarks of Penguin Random House LLC.

StoryBots, Netflix, and all related titles, logos, and characters are trademarks of Netflix, Inc.

Visit us on the Web!
StepIntoReading.com
rhcbooks.com

Educators and librarians, for a variety of teaching tools, visit us at RHTeachersLibrarians.com

ISBN 978-0-593-37387-3 (trade) — ISBN 978-0-593-37388-0 (lib. bdg.) —
ISBN 978-0-593-37389-7 (ebook)

Printed in the United States of America

10 9 8 7 6 5 4 3 2 1

Random House Children's Books supports the First Amendment and celebrates the right to read.

STEP INTO READING®

A SCIENCE READER

STOP THAT VIRUS!

by Scott Emmons
illustrated by Nikolas Ilic

Random House New York

"Oh, my!" says Bing.
"Look over there.
I see a virus in the air!"

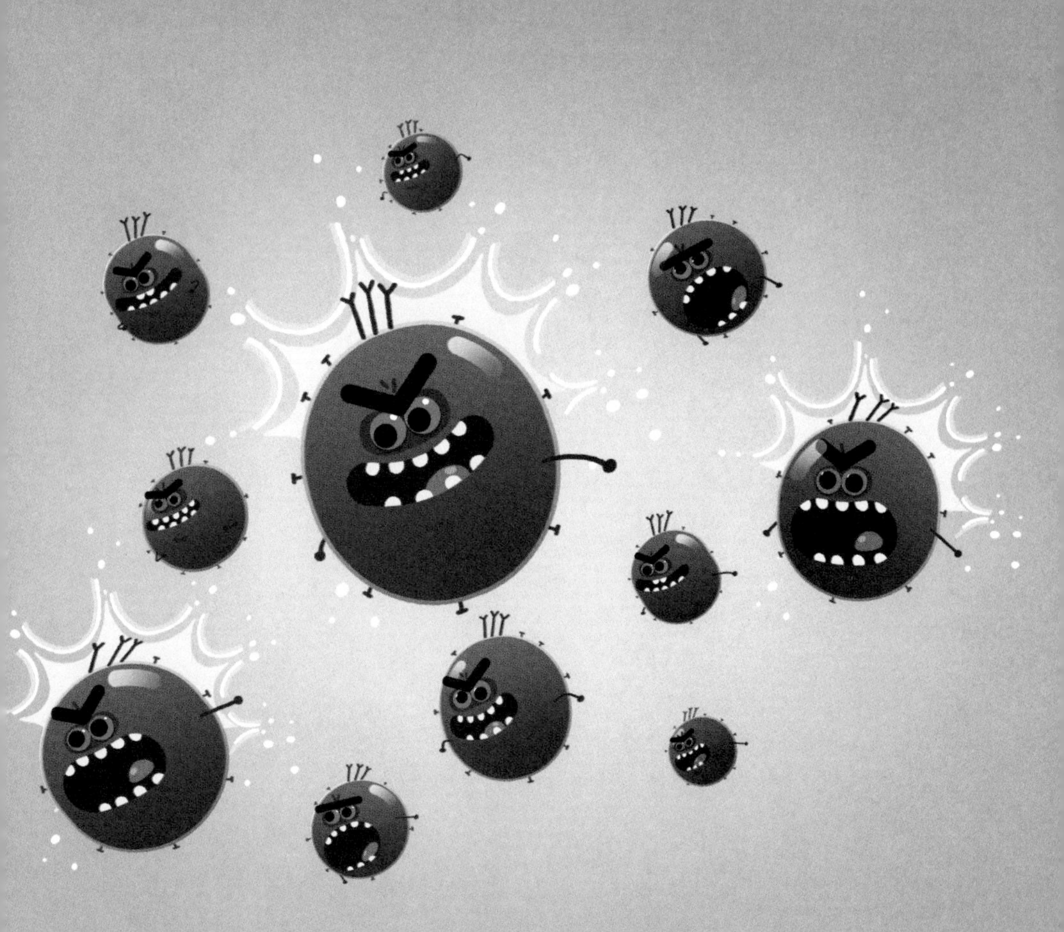

“I see a lot of them,”
says Bo.
“They can make you sick,
you know!”

Now, just what does
a virus do?
It tries to get inside
of you!

And when it does,

it makes you sneeze.

Your throat gets sore.

You cough. You wheeze.

Your nose gets stuffed
and starts to run.
You have a cold.
It is not fun!

But how do viruses
get in
and make a yucky cold
begin?

A floating virus
often lands
in places where
you put your hands.

And when you touch
your mouth or nose,
you bring the virus.
In it goes!

So wash your hands
a lot each day,
and scrub those nasty
germs away.

Use lots of soap!
It does the trick
to help you keep
from getting sick.

But still,

it is so sad to say,

a cold can happen

anyway!

Inside your body,
viruses infect cell by cell,
and soon you do not
feel too well.

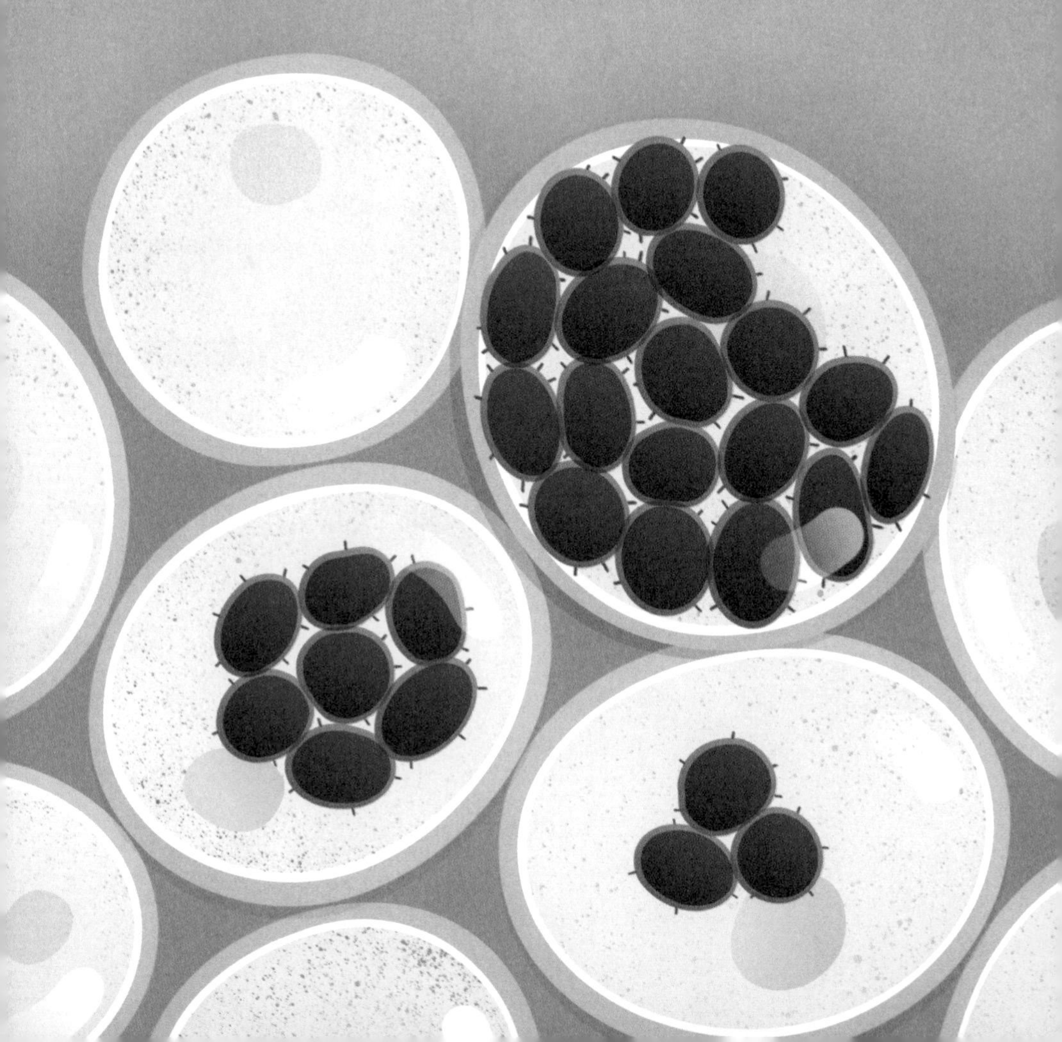

But wait!
White blood cells
then attack and hit
the evil virus back!

And you can help
your body fight
by resting through
the day and night.

A virus is not good to share, so do not spread it in the air.

Any time you cough or sneeze, be sure your mouth is covered, please!

It takes some time
to feel okay.
It does not happen
right away.

Just drink your liquids,
get your rest . . .

. . . and you will
soon be at your best!